EASY
READ
2nd
"S"

-08

Put Beginning Readers on the Right Track with
ALL ABOARD READING™

The All Aboard Reading series is especially designed for beginning readers. Written by noted authors and illustrated in full color, these are books that children really want to read—books to excite their imagination, expand their interests, make them laugh, and support their feelings. With fiction and nonfiction stories that are high interest and curriculum-related, All Aboard Reading books offer something for every young reader. And with four different reading levels, the All Aboard Reading series lets you choose which books are most appropriate for your children and their growing abilities.

Picture Readers

Picture Readers have super-simple texts, with many nouns appearing as rebus pictures. At the end of each book are 24 flash cards—on one side is a rebus picture; on the other side is the written-out word.

Station Stop 1

Station Stop 1 books are best for children who have just begun to read. Simple words and big type make these early reading experiences more comfortable. Picture clues help children to figure out the words on the page. Lots of repetition throughout the text helps children to predict the next word or phrase—an essential step in developing word recognition.

Station Stop 2

Station Stop 2 books are written specifically for children who are reading with help. Short sentences make it easier for early readers to understand what they are reading. Simple plots and simple dialogue help children with reading comprehension.

Station Stop 3

Station Stop 3 books are perfect for children who are reading alone. With longer text and harder words, these books appeal to children who have mastered basic reading skills. More complex stories captivate children who are ready for more challenging books.

In addition to All Aboard Reading books, look for All Aboard Math Readers™ (fiction stories that teach math concepts children are learning in school); All Aboard Science Readers™ (nonfiction books that explore the most fascinating science topics in age-appropriate language); and All Aboard Poetry Readers™ (funny, rhyming poems for readers of all levels).

All Aboard for happy reading!

For Nily—D.S.

For Mom, who always welcomed
the pets that followed me home—A.S.

In loving memory of Skippy, Mr. Diamonds, Clyde, Nudgy, Mazik,
Scratch, Sniff, Aqua, Flame, and Princess—D.S.

Text copyright © 2005 by David Steinberg. Illustrations copyright © 2005 by Adrian C. Sinnott. All rights reserved. Published by Grosset & Dunlap, a division of Penguin Young Readers Group, 345 Hudson Street, New York, New York 10014. ALL ABOARD POETRY READER and GROSSET & DUNLAP are trademarks of Penguin Group (USA) Inc. Printed in the U.S.A.

Library of Congress Cataloging-in-Publication Data

Steinberg, David, 1962–
  Club pet and other funny poems / by David Steinberg ; illustrated by Adrian C. Sinnott.
  p. cm. — (All aboard poetry reader. Station stop 2)
  ISBN 0-448-43774-0 — ISBN 0-448-43773-2 (pbk.)
  1. Pets—Juvenile poetry. 2. Animals—Juvenile poetry. 3. Humorous poetry, American. 4. Children's poetry, American. I. Sinnott, Adrian C., ill. II. Title. III. Series.
  PS3619.T47618C58 2005
  811'.6—dc22
    2004017662

ISBN 0-448-43773-2 (pbk)   10 9 8 7 6 5 4 3 2 1

ISBN 0-448-43774-0 (GB)   10 9 8 7 6 5 4 3 2 1

Club Pet

and Other Funny Poems

TODAY'S
SPECIALS

Linguini
with Kibbles

Mouse Mousse

Worms à la mode

by David Steinberg
illustrated by Adrian C. Sinnott

Grosset & Dunlap • New York

Club Pet

If your dog or cat seems stressed,

If your ferret needs a rest,

I might suggest a little getaway.

If your rat's sick of the race,

Pack his swimsuit in a case

And send him for a <u>Club Pet</u> holiday!

It's a tropical sensation,

A top pet destination

For any genus, species, size, or age.

Whether playing in the ocean

Or just lying out with lotion,

Pets'll tell you this resort is all the rage.

The bunny boardwalk band

Is playing Dixieland

As beagles boogie-board on waves of blue.

Mini-poodles in bikinis

Dine on kibbles and linguini

As salamanders paddle a canoe.

If your guppy's feeling blah,

Dunk him in our brand-new spa.

Or treat your python to a facial peel.

Why not try a turtle trike?

Or go for a hamster hike?

There's a thousand things to do here—
what a deal!

What fun we guarantee!

But just you wait and see

How much your pets will miss you
when they're through—

They'll run straight for your gate,

So excited they can't wait

To come back home so they
can be with you!

13

How to Train Your Owner
(For Dogs Only)

Time to train your owner?

I'll tell you what to do:

Grab a ball and wag your tail

And watch— he'll follow you!

Drop that ball into his hand

(Or you can use a stick).

Bark until he throws it.

See <u>that</u>—he's learned a trick!

Make him throw it fifty times

Till he gets the knack;

Every time he throws it,

Bring that ball right back.

Once your owner's learned to throw,

Give that guy a treat.

Put a leash around his hand

And walk him down the street.

If he dawdles on the way

(People are so slow!),

Teach him how to run—

Just tug that leash and <u>GO</u>!

When he's running for his life,

Stop to sniff a bush.

Just watch—he'll learn to "heel"

After landing on his tush!

If your food bowl's empty,

Just scrape it 'cross the floor.

Or teach him how to let you out

By scratching at the door.

What a day of training!

What promise that guy shows!

Now let him know how proud you are—

Jump up and lick his nose!

Mr. MacKay's Macaw

Mr. MacKay's got a Marvelous Pet—

The smartest Macaw that you ever MacMet.

She Sits on his Head, giving him a MacNuzzle

Each Morning as he does his Crossword MacPuzzle,

And when Old MacKay gets MacStuck for a Word,

She Squawks out the Answer, that clever MacBird!

She'll tell you how many MacHoles
on the Moon

Or Name the MacMan who invented
the Spoon.

She Knows each MacPresident's Birthday
by Heart,

So How—you MacAsk—did she get so
MacSmart?

Quite Simple, you see—after Mr. MacKay

Puts the Lining inside her MacCage
every day,

That Macaw just MacSits on her little
MacSeat

And MacReads the MacNewspaper
under her Feet!

Stunt Cat

From Katmandu to Catalina,

No cat's as famous as Felina.

That cat's far out. That cat's so groovy.

That cat's the star of her own movie.

34

She plays a spy. She leaps. She flies

Off speeding trains—take <u>that</u>, bad guys!

She spins and kicks and saves the world

Without a lick of fur unfurled!

And if you ask, "How <u>does</u> she do it?"

She'll just purr, "Ahhh, nothing to it."

But let me tell you, boys and girls,

While that Felina primps her curls,

While she's off living like a queen,

It's <u>me</u> you're watching on the screen!

It's me and not that spoiled brat!

It's me, the underpaid <u>stunt cat</u>!

When any scene is too much trouble,

She shouts, "Cut! Go get my double!"

That's my cue—I'm tossed her hat

And take my place as her stunt cat.

I jump and fall and take the blows—

It's me who gets punched in the nose.

I'm bounced and trounced around the set

Till I can hardly call the vet.

But when we watch the final edit,

Guess which cat gets <u>all</u> the credit?

Guess who stands to take the bow?

Whose smile endorses Kitty Chow?

Who's served imported milk and cheese?

Which cat's sent touring overseas?

Who's this year's Best Cat nominee?

One thing's for sure, it isn't—

BRRRRING!

Mee-ow? Mee-ow? Hello? What's <u>that</u>?

Why yes, it's me, the stunt spy cat.

Felina's hiking through Peru?

She won't come back for "Spy Cat Two"?

So you want <u>me</u>? Now <u>I'm</u> the star?

I get her trailer? Chef? Town car?!

Well, I might just agree to that . . .

If you throw in my <u>own</u> stunt cat!

Gerbil Gym

Is your fur a little flabby?

Feeling out of shape a bit?

Has your waggy tail turned saggy?

Gerbil Gym will get you fit!

Stop lounging by the food dish—

Get up and move that tail!

Come scamper twenty laps

In our Fabbo-Habitrail!

Then take a midnight run

On our Turbo Gerbo-Wheel,

Named "X-treme X-erciser"

In this month's <u>PETS OF STEEL</u>!

Believe me, I was once like you—

A puny rodent punk!

But thanks to Gerbil Gym,

You can be . . .

a gerbil-hunk!